Hustler's Bustle

A fictional life story of Mmbuka; a self-made hustler who rose through a challenging African childhood, the struggles, and navigating around it all to be a successful impactful leader

By

Sisco Mbindi

DISCLAIMER

This is a fictional account of life experiences of a self-made hustler, growing from a humble beginning, fighting against the odds to emerge victorious. All the characters and their experiences, organizations and events portrayed in this story are fictional but a depiction of real life realities in this part of the world.

First Edition, August, 2018.

Preface

Nothing is set on stone. The dynamics of life keep changing and you have to adapt to the changes. Mmbuka did not expect the world to change on him. When it did he was not ready for the hurdles he had to jump over in order to get to where he wanted to be.

He never expected to be uprooted from his family home to go live upcountry with his grandparents. He rejected that idea from the very beginning. He tried to stay in a world of make believe so that he could postponed his reality.

He finally got his wake up call and nothing could bring him down now.

This is a story of a young man who fights against the odds to emerge victorious. Mmbuka works hard to destroy the notion, that he was destined to fail because his life had changed. He had a secret life that he wished he could have but living upcountry made it seem far out of reach. He set his mind to one thing and worked towards ensuring that he did not let his circumstance define his journey.

This story answers the question of what if circumstances would go differently, what would you do?

Hustler's Bustle

Chapter One

This is it. This is where it all began. As you grow up, you never notice the things that are being held together by glue that isn't strong enough. There are so many cracks, but you choose to look past them.

Everything is perfect. That's what life looks like when you are a child living like a child. You are oblivious to the realities around you. Your parents are in love with each other. Even the bickering sounds like loving words to you. Your siblings annoy you, and you imagine why you couldn't have been the only child. But then you imagine a life without them, and it looks very bleak.

In as much as you would like to pretend otherwise you actually like school and mathematics is your favorite subject. Playing with your friends is the highlight of your day. You get to eat on a daily basis. You never know where the money comes from, but you are always asking for something.

My fondest memory as a child was when my father would come back home from work. He worked in another town so we would mostly see him on the weekends. We would see our full of life Peugeot 504 pulling up to our apartment building. That car was old, but my dad loved it because he bought it with a fortune of his savings.

My brothers and I would pretend we could drive it. We were untouchable the children in the estate would envy us. My father's car was the only one there. The key was never in the ignition, but my father promised us that one-day we would get to drive it. Kibisu my elder brother would get lessons when my father was in a good mood, and we were always jealous. The perks of being the eldest but pretend driving was always a delight.

My dad would immediately get out of the car to carry Inyaya his youngest baby. We would rush to carry whatever he had in the car. He would always bring us something even if it were just sweets. It was a simple life.

My parents were teachers, but they made the ends meet with the money they got. It wasn't like we were leaving in a mansion, but life was good. I cannot describe how that simplicity felt like heaven to me as I grew up. The moment you cannot afford even to drink water is when you long for the things you took for granted.

There was this song that my parents played whenever they were having an argument. I never noticed it until my brother pointed it out to me. We called it the arguing song. I remember when he bought that; my mother did not look as excited as we did. We could not sleep; we had a car now. That night that song was played.

Nothing prepares you for change especially if the illusion of perfection has been edged into your mind.

"Get out, *nimechoka* I can't keep doing this," she said.

(Nimechoka- I am tired)

"Mama Kibisu calm down the kids will hear you," he retorted. My siblings and I were in the sitting room. Nekesa was asleep. I felt like we were invading their privacy. I still had that childlike wonder, and I was disappointed that they did not put the arguing song on. I was in school half the time and I still had the notion that everything was okay.

One of my brothers was tiptoeing towards their bedroom. But my elder brother would not allow it. He walked towards Cazentar who my immediate follower was and pulled him back to the sitting room.

Now we had to pretend that we were watching the movie keenly. Yet, all we wanted to know was what was going on in that bedroom.

"And so what?" she said. Then my father mumbled something that we could not hear then the door was opened.

"If you do not get out willingly, I will throw your things outside." My siblings and I could hear everything, but we stayed silent. Praying that it was nothing serious. When my father walked out of the bedroom with a suitcase, I knew that prayer did not go through. Like I said my dad was a weekend father due to his nature of work. He always had luggage with him but nothing as huge as a suitcase. My mum would always go see him during the week to ensure that he had clothes and other necessities for his house at work place. My father just walks out without saying a word to us. It was like we were none existent. We watch him from the window. He kicked the car door and dropped the suitcase. He came back in because he forgot the car keys. He picked them and walked out with frown face without a word.

We all scamper to the door as he turns the ignition on and drove away. We didn't cry. We just look on wondered what was going on.

My elder brother has always been like a father figure to us ever since. He was just about to finish university. He always seemed to know what to do when things were not okay. We all turn to look at him for the way forward. I was just about to finish high school, but I had been shielded from many things on the home front. I could take care of myself, but I had my family there, so I did not have to put those skills to test often. I was surviving a boy's high school that meant I could get myself out of situations.

We stayed silent we all walked back to our seats. My elder brother instructed us to go to sleep. My four younger brothers walked to their bedroom. I pretended that I was walking to the room we shared with Kibisu. I saw him walking towards my parents' bedroom. He knocked and as soon as he went in. I went to the door and just stood there. I could hear her sobbing.

"Everything is going to be okay mum," said Kibisu. Was it going to be okay? Or was he just saying that to keep her calm? I was not in the loop, and I desperately needed to know what was happening. And yet at that moment as I stood outside my mother's door and imagined the hardship we starred facing as my father's disappearance downed! Considering he was our breadwinner despite mum being a board teacher I knew something worse was about to change our life style in to oblivion unless he came back. Days past, weeks went by months counted, our father never came back, and things turned upside down. I started feeling the vacuum. Many essentials started being rationed and even diminishing and life became harder day by day.

Chapter Two

The cock crowing right next to me startles me. I wondered why I always thought of my past like that a city boy forever with all I desired. I needed to move on to adopt to the hard change, but I was engulfed in thoughts of the city before breakup of my parents which haunted me for quite some time even in my dreams before I could adjust.

After some months, reality of life heat was evident. My mother was unable to meet our needs including normal provision and cater for other housing bills. We at times slept on empty stomach and yawned all nights. Our health started deteriorating and we became unhappy with millions of thoughts in the city where everything given freely to us by Dad became payable. We had to tighten the rope by skipping some meals. It was a turmoil state of affair which my mother could not take it any more since all dreams were closed in this very trying times.

It was time to make drastic decision to retreat to the locality where she thought mercy would be lenient to our status and grant us comfort. This was to be our grandparents help to salvage our perthitic situation.

Imagine finding yourself there with everything that you had grown accustomed to nowhere in sight like a flash. At my grandparents I was sleeping on the floor now with a mattress that was a half inch thick thus like sleeping on the empty floor. I always wake up so tired out of discomfort.my body still complained little by little when I had to wake up at that time. I had no choice but slowly to get used to my new life.

I was full of sorrow, cried deep down my thoughts wondering how we came down this far, always wake up so tired with ever unending deem thoughts.

It was around five in the morning. I had to wake up at that time to the good news that I had passed my secondary examination to attend university course. I, however was slowly getting used to my new life in the locality.

I was so excited and collected my admission letter for my university. I was in additional thoughts wondering who will help me out to foot my college fee. These was hard puzzle to crack and all the time, first thing I always did was to take out my admission letter to the university read it. I would read through my calling letter admitted in university to do a course in actuarial science.

As I adopted to the local lifestyle having passed my examinations. The first thing I always did was to take out my admission letter to the university. It was my reminder that there was more to this life.

I would read through it my; I was admitted for the course in actuarial science. I was good in mathematics. It came naturally to me. I know people hate people who make statements like those. Calculating sums and looking at problems was therapeutic to me. That calling letter was my prized possession at that point in my life. It gave me hope. Hope was my opium, and I never wanted to be weaned off it.

I was staying with my grandparents now. It changed how I saw the world after experiencing rough times. Life change and all was different. Nothing was being handed to me as my dad used to. Work had to be done.

I walked out of my makeshift room next to my grandparents' house. I shared that room with my cousin Mudaki who was on a drinking spree most of the time. He did not come last night, and I could not wait to hear the stories from his drinking escapades.

The one thing that always got me was the sunrise with warms in Itando. It was different from what I experienced in the city. Every morning I woke up and I saw the sunrise I had hope for a better day even if it just lasted a microsecond. I was holding on to moments that would make me forget about the situation at hand.

My grandparents were struggling to make ends meet, being too old it was difficult for them to farm and fend for themselves. I could not blame them. They were not planning on raising another child when my mother sent me to them. I was a burden placed on them. They would never admit that but when you have more mouths to feed without an income can make you look older.

I could hear them praying for the entire family and our situation of breakup of my mum and dad, that was their routine. The moment I had the Amen. I walked in. My grandfather was the only one seated on their two-sitter couch that belonged to my parents when they were living in a smaller house before going to Nakuru for teaching job.

"*Habari ya asubuhi babu*?"

(Good morning grandfather)

He would always place his hand on my head when we met in the morning. It was his way of blessing me. I felt reassured with that gesture. We exchanged pleasantries as we waited for breakfast.

"Huyo Mudaki alirudi nyumbani kweli?"

(Is Mudaki back yet?)

We laughed because we both knew the answer to that. He had gotten a regular job, and he was paid a handful which he directed to the bottle. He would not come back until every cent was spent. That was his daily routine. Then he would come to tell us that he would not touch alcohol again. That was followed by his go-to phrase *'inaharibu maisha'*(It ruins your life).

"Usikuwe kama huyo kijana."

(Don't be like that boy)

I nodded in agreement because that was like the mantra in this house and it was even repeated in the presence of Madaki.

My grandmother walked in with a flask that most probably had porridge in it. She was always smiling despite the circumstances surrounding us. When she smiled it just warmed your heart.

She was holding two cups for my grandfather and me. She just smiled at me.

"Kula mtoto wangu."

(Eat my child)

"Asante mum," I said. (Thank you mum)

She walked back to the kitchen. It was just a small area partitioned in the house. It had most of her utensils because if she left them in the outdoor kitchen, they could be stolen.

I knew that she woke up earlier than all of us in order to ensure that we had something to put in our bellies before we headed out to the farm or in locality to seek errant jobs for a fee.

I had another cousin, Makungu who was in high school. She always left early because she had to walk to school daily. She spent most of her time at home than in school due to lack of school fees most of the session, but my grandmother courageously would go to the school and beg for her to be allowed in class while looking for money.

Begging was her specialty at this point. She even begged to get flour. She begged to get paraffin etc. There was nothing she would not beg for just to ensure that our life was a bit better for the day confrontation. I had started calling her mum because it just felt right. She reminded me of my mum as well. She was the very definition of the heart of gold. Positive vibes even when it would be easier to be negative.

We would be heading to the shamba with my grandfather after our meal. There after my activities in the farm, I would head to the village center to try and find some odd jobs.

There was no variety in meals while I was there. Porridge was the staple breakfast with sweet potatoes. Bread was a luxury I had long forgotten. Lunch was usually reserved for those who were in the house, and it was usually

Mabwoni(sweet potatoes), *mabwoni* was dinner as well. Ugali was there as well with traditional vegetables. I loathed them when I was with my mum.

"I don't want *Saga(traditional bitter vegetable)* mummy."

She would mumble things in the kitchen, but in the long run, she would make me something different. I tried pulling that stunt with my grandmother. She just smiled and walked away. From that day I knew that the only option I had was what was on the table.

It took a while for me to adjust but you could not want something that was not there. It was a matter of survival. I realized in locality poverty varied hence as much we were in poor state, we were one of the lucky ones. Some in the neighborhood would literally go to bed hungry.

I took my porridge there was a hint of sugar. I smiled. I knew that it was going to be a good day. I finished my breakfast and went outside to wait for my grandfather. At this point, I knew he only followed me to the shamba just to feel useful. His bones were weak. Lifting a jembe was an uphill task. I liked his resilience.

He woke up every morning and followed me to the shamba. He stayed with me till the work for the day was done. He would tell me stories of the past and all the dreams he had.

He wasn't much of a talker. Just like me, I was named after him. It is assumed in our culture that you tend to pick a couple of traits from the person you are named after. Our time in the shamba (farm), however, showed me a different side of him. He could be very animated when he talked about his past. It made the work easier because you are occupied by something else as you worked.

Every season is different on the farm. During this season we were harvesting the maize. This was marking an anniversary for me because I came to them during the same season. I was thrown in the water without any floaters. The only thing I had seen close to a shamba was my mum's small kitchen garden.

My grandmother used to come to the farm with us and laugh at how I was harvesting the maize. I have the battle scars to prove that I was once a novice in that field. She broke her back. I think she misses the farm it was her language. Even though she was old, she actually enjoyed her time with the crops.

By now you know we could not afford to machines for the harvesting process. We would try to finish the work before the sun was fully out. Once the sun was out the speed of labor lowered.

I would take the farm tools back to the house because my grandfather could not carry them by himself. During my working on the farm I never went back in the house because my grandmother would start telling stories that would slow down my day in the farm.

"Babu naenda kutafuta kibarua nitarudi jioni."

(I am going to look for work; I will be back in the evening)

I waved him goodbye and walked towards the village center after turning up from the farm. I was going to look for something to do. I wasn't uncouth, but the village life could change someone. I was trying to dispute the notions that when in Rome you have to do what the Romans do. I was just doing best to ensure that I had a fighting chance in the environment that I found myself in. I, however, was still trying to hold to the fragments of the life I was accustomed to. They called me *mtu wa town* (city boy) even as I looked for jobs that would be a hindrance at first. They would touch my hands and tell me that these hands had not seen life. Trying to convince them that I needed that job would fall on deaf ears. I was determined; there was something I was fighting for and no amount of intimidation could have put me off.

My first attempt at working in the construction industry was a disaster. I was a source of entertainment for the men and women there. You had a target that you needed to get to in a day in order to get a decent amount of money. Your masculinity would be brought into question once you stood next to the men on the site. Some would carry bricks on their backs without flinching. The amount of food they ate equated the amount of work they did. The calluses I got from that made my hands rough, and from that moment I was accepted in a way.

There were days I would go back home with as little as 50 shillings, and that would count as a good day. The many people we worked with would say no today, and I would be there the next day, I think it wore them down. My persistence could be nagging, but that was the only choice I did when it came to my mind I had to find myself a step in to the future.

I was trying to save up for college knowing very well all depended on my cards on the table. The only thing that was stopping me was money. I would do anything to attain a university degree. I was almost meeting my mark. I was called in under the joint admission board. I would get a subsidy in my school fees as well as the higher education loan board after enrolling. All I needed was just to get my feet through the door.

I was heading to my first gig of the day, at a construction site. It was never a guarantee that you would get a job there. When I started, I would just walk around the village hoping that you would come across a site.

We were casuals. We had no right to demand a lot of money. You would be lucky if you could get a foreman who was empathetic to the situation surrounding the area. Most of the constructions jobs were from city people. They had the most money. I was going to lay bricks and mix the cement. If someone had told me that that was the direction my life was taking. I would never have believed them. The job requires strength that I did not believe could come from me. But when you are pushed to a corner, you summon up energy that was always inside you but was not being used. I met good people there who were fighting for something as well. Everyone had a different story but what amazed me is they did not let their circumstances bring them down. I had it good for a while and when things changed I almost fell apart. They gave me hope. Most of them were just doing this to achieve the bare minimum, ensure that their children do not go to bed hungry. Put a roof over their head just for the night. Every battle was different, but we all hoped that we would emerge victorious.

The foreman in this site was friendly, and you could walk away with at least five hundred in that day. That was a hallelujah moment for me. That meant I could give some to my grandparents and the other amount would go into my savings. I did not think of spending it on luxuries just the necessary things needed. There were days I would see a bottle of soda and crave it. Then I looked at the bigger picture, and I would not succumb to my cravings. There were days I would just go and drink it. Just so that I would not forget how it tasted like.

The project was almost over, so I was just counting days till I had to find something else. There was nothing I had not done at that point in my life. I used to sell charcoal. That was one of the most lucrative jobs I ever had while I was in the village. We mostly depended on outside customers because the locals can look for alternative means for fuel that does not make out a dent in their pockets.

I was a tout for the matatus that plied that route. I thought that it was an easy job because it does not involve a lot of manual labor. I was so wrong. Being a tout, I like being in the customer service industry. You meet different people with different emotions. I cannot count the number of times I lost money because I was not keen enough. Of course, they would recover the money from my wages. Some other clients were very rude, and it would take everything in you not to lose your cool. We would carry excess passengers and I would think that this was wrong. I however had no right to say a thing. Once I lost that job, I did not feel dejected. I had become street smart I knew how to navigate my way in the village.

I was growing accustomed to the life that was handed over to me, but it was not rosy. I once got a job where I was expected to man a farm during the night hours. I was robbed as they harvested the contents of the farm. I tried screaming for help, but no one came to my rescue. I have never been scared in my life. I felt like everything that I was working for was flashing right before my eyes. I couldn't fight back. I cowered down when they kicked me but when they realized I was not a threat.

In the morning as the owner of the farm was assessing the damage, I thought I would be blamed for it. He was a reasonable man.

"Mmbuka usijali hao watu tutapata hii wiki tu heri hawakukudhuru," he said with certainty.

(We will get those men this week do not worry, is even good they didn't harm you)

Despite the assurance; I could not continue since the fear in me was biting me all over. I quit that job the next day after I explained what happened to my grandparents. I was not willing to die for money that would not get me the far I aspired if I lost my life. In the evening I would get home and head to the kitchen directly. I would be famished by the time I got to the house after long nights of empty stomach. I tried to understand why people in the village ate so early. I think it is because they want to sleep their sorrows away. Then wake up and face the next day with new resolve.

"Mumeshindaje?" (How have you been?) I asked as soon as I entered the main house. My grandparents were preparing themselves to go to sleep. My cousin was working on her schoolwork. She would have to wash the dishes first before going to sleep and ensuring that she has made preparations for the next day.

I would walk to my grandmother and place a folded note in her hand. She would smile, and at that moment I knew that everything would be better.

"*Laleni vizuri,*" (Goodnight) they said as they headed to their bedroom.

As I started eating, I thought of the lessons I learnt while I stayed with my grandparents. I learnt how to be selfless. The very art of knowing that you can be kind to people in the smallest way and it will just make your day better. Patience is another lesson I learnt. I was used to things going my way immediately. Now I know that it might take more time than I would like to admit but I was certain that it would happen eventually.

We had a short conversation with my cousin, and I headed to the room I shared with Mudaki. I got in expecting the strong stench of alcohol to welcome me. But he still was not back. He usually stayed out for three days maximum this was day two, so we would be expecting him the next day.

Before I slept, I always read out my mantra. I got it from one of the books my mother gave me. I did not know who wrote the words.

> *Forget everything about your past, start afresh and allow the lessons learnt to guide me to my present, which I have total control over.*

It helped me think about the future. There were days when I woke up, and sunlight was beating through the window, but it didn't feel bright. Because I could be in sunlight but still be in darkness. I hated those days, but I managed to pull through because I was here still fighting.

Routines gave me something to look forward to. An idle mind would lead to drinking, and I wanted no part of that life. I did not want to be a statistic of someone who had potential but gave up because they could not fight the vices in the environment he found himself in.

Chapter Three

As I drifted off to sleep that night, there was only one thing on my mind. My mother. My thoughts went right back to hard times before I relocated to grandparents.

At that time, she had already moved into the school compound in a one roomed cube following her inability to afford to pay rent for our house in the town which led to our eviction then. It was not a bad adjustment for her though things were tough.

Having cleared loans for educating my elder brother. That meant that at least there was a surplus to cater for my other sibling's needs, but it was still hard. The house was not enough that's all I can say. The compound was spacious, and I could just walk around when I children were in class and go back in our cube; I could see she was struggling being untrained teacher the pay was less lucrative. She had one less mouth to feed, and that was Kibisu who had joined my sister in the city to look for a job. But she still had five more to think of in the new uncomfortable settlement. Raising seven children is not an easy task on an untrained teacher's salary.

I knew that my father stopped assisting her the day he left now ages ago. I heard my mum and Kibisu arguing about it. The last time I saw my dad was when he furiously drove off after unknown quarrel broke and left with his suitcase and the car. I learnt he showed up when we had gone to church and took everything he had bought. And by his things, I mean literally everything that he had bought. My mum rushed back home to try to beg him to return but no, he left her the television, and I know his heart softened on television because of Inyanya.

At this point, the wrinkles on my mother's face were becoming more pronounced. I had finished my secondary examination hoping to pass and join campus, and I kept reminding her of it every waking moment that she prepare to push me to the next level. I was selfish. I could see the situation around us. I was not willing to give up on my dreams. Kibisu could not finish university when hardship fell on us, yet I felt like I was entitled to that opportunity because I was certain to excel in final examinations.

He was doing odd jobs in Nairobi, and he sent whatever he could. But he was surviving, and there was only so much he could do.

It is hard to forget the night she told me that I had to go stay with my grandparents. I was in the kitchen; I was clearing the dishes from the sink. I had to wait for her to get to the house because she had extra classes just to supplement the income she got.

I heard the door opening, but I did not rush to receive her. I wanted to finish doing the dishes.

"Mmbuka, I need to speak to you."

I could hear the fatigue in her voice. She was straining. I dried my hands then went to the sitting room.

"Yes, mum."

I sat next to her. I did not expect any heavy conversation. It might have been an explanation of what was required of me the next day. But she was not looking at me.

"What's wrong?" I asked.

"I have tried my best Mmbuka, but I can't do it."

I was about to interrupt her, but she gestured for me to stop.

"You have to go live with my parents, once things get better you can come back."

There was finality in her voice that assured me that this was not up for debate. When she was married to my dad, I think I only saw her parents once.

"What about school?" I stuttered.

"Not now my son."

She went to the bedroom she shared with Inyanya. That was it. I wanted to cry, but I was a man. Or at least that's what I thought. I needed to take this without a chip on my shoulder, but I did the exact opposite.

I wondered how I would ever be the same again, not even as a man but as a human being.

"I know you are mad at me right now, but I am doing this for you."

At that time I used to sleep in the living room to create space for my siblings. I could not sleep. I prayed that my mother was just kidding. Even while I prayed, I knew that this was a shut case. I did not even ask when I was leaving. I thought that if I ignored my impending departure long enough, it might not come to fruition.

I was in denial. Can you believe that she packed my clothes for me? One evening I had gone out to play football with my friends. I get to the house to find a suitcase packed placed in the corner of the living room.

"Inyanya whose bag is that?"

For a split second, I thought that my dad was back and I would not have to leave. Your mind plays tricks on you especially when you do not want to accept the reality.

"Mmbuka njoo," she said. (Mmbuka come here)

I walked to her bedroom. I was dragging my feet. We had not been speaking since she broke the news to me. She told me that I would be traveling to my grandparent the next day. It was no discussion just the passing of information from one individual to another. Everything she was saying was like gibberish to me.

"Someone will pick you up once you alight at Itando. Please understand that I am doing this for you."

I walked out without saying a word. Before I knew it, I was in Itando starting my new life.

For a while, I was mad at her for sending me to her parents. It was during one of my conversations with my grandmother that I learnt that my mum had lost her a job. Moved out of the schoolhouse. She had sent my younger brothers

Akiza and Isinga to stay with one of her siblings. She stayed with the other children as she was looking for a job. I wondered why she did not tell me. I think it would have been easier for me to handle it if I knew the backstory. She did not want me to be pressurized.

There were days I wanted to write myself off. I felt like the hand that used to give me was the same hand that took away from me. I wanted to go to school my ambitions would not give me peace despite the situation I was in. Take my rightful share of life by force. I regretted how I dealt with my mother because she was literally breaking her back so that I could not lack a thing.

Separation from my siblings was killing me. I was used to having around me. It is obvious there were days that we would not get along. However, the good days outweighed the bad

In the realms of my fantasy, I go back to the day my dad walked out. He would not have left, and we would not be here. I would run out of headspaces. My mind would be tangled in the version of reality that I wanted.

It is a one-day at a time journey. If you rush you take short cuts that you will end up regretting. That is why I only dealt with the problem that each day presented. Yes my eyes were set on something. My goal was dependent on how each day went.

I believe that if I did not approach my situation that way I would be unable to get out of the trenches. You cannot predict how life unfolds. If we had that super power then maybe we would quickly change the tough times that were ahead of us. Now I believe that those tough times shape you. It just depended on the spectrum that you viewed it from. I did not want to allow myself to become a pointless existence. I could feel it in my being that I was meant to bring change. The problem was in what aspect.

Chapter Four

I could see that the sun had not risen yet I knew it was morning. My body clock that I had spent my life refining was getting good at not failing me. I checked my beat up watch that my father gave me. It was like a momentum of the time we had spent together and I did not want to let it go. The watch was informing that it was time to wake up.

I felt like my room was staring back at me. It was looking through me and seeing my secrets that I did not want to reveal. It was just me and my room. What was it trying to tell me? I felt like it was calling me out. It was urging me to rise up and proceed to make a change in my life. It was time for me to start thinking about heading to Nairobi. However I something was still holding me to the floor as if something was lying on top of me. I knew what was holding me back it was the money.

I closed my eyes pretending that I could conjure up sleep. I could not get any rest; I could feel my heart beat loud and insistent. It was invading force that did not understand that things were not always in black and white. When the sound of my heartbeat was interrupted by approaching footsteps outside I was relieved. I could hear someone humming and it was getting closer to my door. I opened my eyes and for some reason I felt ready for my day.

It was Mudaki finally coming back home after a drinking spree. I could not quite place the song he was humming but from that moment I knew that it would be in my thoughts for the better part of the day.

I would have liked to stay and listen to his escapades. It would have slowed me down. As I walked out of my room heading to the bathroom area I bumped into him.

"My brother I see you have finally decided to come home."

He pulled me closer and whispered in my year.

"I did not forget you, I carried a little something for you."

He said that as he opened his jacket. I could see he had a quarter bottle of the cheap liquor he used to consuming. I just laughed because there was no point in arguing with him at that moment.

"Keep it safe for me, I will come back for it in the evening."

I walked a way before it turned into a story telling session. As I rushed past him the stench of a brewery followed me. I just shook my head. When Wafula was drunk my grandfather would be angered. However he has simmered down now because he knows Wafula is the only person who can change his attitude.

Sharing a room with another grown man was something I had to adjust to. Mudaki was older than me and according to the African culture he deserved more respect. I always had to carry everything I needed when I headed to the bathroom. It was rusty old iron sheet building that was put beside the house. I would always think of tetanus shots when I walked into it. I got cut once. I think I exaggerated it a bit but it was dangerous. However you make due with the situation at hand. I would tell myself that once I get money I would build my grandparents a bathroom.

I was already fully dressed by the time I left the bathroom. I went back to the room to return my towel. I did not want to go into the main house. I was rushing to my construction job.

I was willing to sacrifice at least thirty shillings on that day for a meal .the good thing about that meal is that it could take me through the whole day.

I went to the site for the last day. They were clearing the area to ensure that it was ready for occupancy. The foreman gave me that job because I had told him my story. I was lucky to get that job.

My faith in humanity was restored by his kind gesture. He was not obligated to offer me that job but he did. Maybe my begging was a contributing factor but I had the job nonetheless.

I would quantify that day as one of my easiest working day. It was a five bedroomed house for an upcoming politician. I was there with three other men and we divided the labor amongst ourselves. We would prioritize with the interior then finish the exterior. All the work needed to be finished on that day.

I did not even notice as time elapsed; it was getting close to five in the afternoon. There was a hooting at the gate but we ignored it since the foreman had not instructed us of any visitors. The person with the car was very persistent. I rushed to the gate because I was the youngest. On opening the gate it was the foreman and the 'mheshimiwa' (honorable). He was on his path to prominence and that meant a title came with it. They drove in and I had to wait for them to park before I could go back into the house.

When the 'mheshimiwa' walked out of the car with foreman. I just could not believe it. He did not look as old as I had expected. I had this notion of a how a politician is supposed to look like. Fat, pot bellied, receding hair line and have this air around him. This makes them think that they are better than us. He was different. He reminded me of my elder brother.

He had hope in his eyes. I know you are going to ask me how I can see hope? I do not know how I can possibly describe it. He seemed like he believed in the ideologies he was spreading around town. He had the house built so that he could 'connect' with the constituents. I commend him for that step but the only way he could connect with us was by talking to us.

I highly doubt a mansion can be a conversation starter for someone who is struggling to put just one meal on the table.

"Kijana come and greet the mheshimiwa," the foreman beckoned.

I rushed to their side. We exchanged pleasantries as he asked about the progress of the work.

"We are about to begin clearing the compound," I answered. The foreman instructed me to begin clearing the compound as the headed inside to inspect the house.

I had to separate the materials that were still in good shape from the ones that should be discarded. People who cannot afford can reuse the ones that should have been discarded. Once they pay us for the day we would divide the materials amongst ourselves.

When they finally walked out the mheshimiwa looked content with work being done.

"We will bring the furniture tomorrow. Find two serious workers who would be willing to help me move in."

He got into his car and waved at me. I smiled. At that moment I felt a tad bit important. The foreman opened the gate for him as he left.

He came back to me smiling from ear to ear.

"Your stars have just aligned my boy."

I did not understand what he meant by that.

"He wants you to come back tomorrow, that means more money for you."

It took all that I had in me not to break out in song and dance.

"Thank you so much," I said.

He tried to pretend that he was not as excited for me but I could see that he was happy. From the moment I started working there he had been sympathetic to my situation. He would encourage me not to give up on my dream .He did not owe me anything but I appreciated his generosity towards me.

I could only reiterate what he stated. I could feel the stars were aligning for me. I could not take things for granted.

Once we cleared the compound the foreman gave us our dues. I passed by the market that day and bought meat. Meat had become a luxury. I was so excited as I went home with my paper bag with a quarter kilogram of beef. I knew that the meat would be full of soup. Getting even two pieces of meat was exciting.

I knew my grandmother would complain. She always did that even when I gave her money.

"No, haufai kuwaste pesa zako hivyo." (No, don't waste your money on me.)

"I am not wasting it if I am giving it to you mama."

She finally stopped bothering me about it. That's why I always forced it into her hands. It would be a constant debate if I did not do that.

I got home earlier than usual. I went straight to the kitchen and found my grandmother making ugali.

I took a seat next to her and handed her the paper bag containing the meat.

"Hii ni nini?" (What is this?)

I started laughing and asked her to check inside. She just smiled. That smile that makes everything seem right with the world.

"You didn't have to do that," she said.

I walked to the door and just smiled at her. I went to my room. I was now ready to listen to every story that Wafula had. I opened it expecting to find him on the wooden chair. He was not there.

I took my envelopes and looked through my admission letter. The deadline for me to accept the offer was fast approaching.

I had called the school to tell them that I would be reporting a bit later. I was lucky that they allowed a certain grace period so that I could organize myself.

I had one more month to get my things in order. The next semester was about to begin and I needed to start thinking about how I would be getting to Nairobi.

I was still short of cash and I did not know where I could scrap up the remaining amount. It felt like one thing was working and then something else was falling apart. I was deep in my thoughts urging my being not to write myself of yet. I had just taken a sit trying to calculate how I could get to my target amount when I heard my cousin call out my name.

It was time for supper. The sun was still out. We decided to eat on the verandah. I liked it when we took our meals together. It used to be a rule in our house. We all had to eat together. It was our bonding time. At my grandmothers it was different everyone ate when they arrived from work or when they felt like it. There were days I preferred it to what I was accustomed to at home. And then there were days I wanted to share my thoughts with someone and ended up just staying silent.

We talked about our day. My grandfather even made fun of me.

"We have an important man in our midst, if we can afford meat things are changing," he said. That kept us laughing during dinner.

I helped my cousin to clear the dishes after dinner. This was so she could go and study. I had come home earlier than usual and I was not as fatigued.

I later found out that Wafula had gone to his girlfriend. He was what we referred to as 'Kiguu na Njia'. He was never settled staying in the house was not an option for him ever.

I understood him. Being alone with your thoughts could make you go crazy especially in the environment we were in.

I saw my cousin walking out with two cups to add to the utensils.

"Shosho says you should go see them once you are done."

We had two kitchens one was for storage and light cooking. The other was meant for cooking every other thing. We had a rack just outside the 'bigger kitchen' where we dried the utensils. The rule was that once the dishes were dry everything had to be taken to my grandmothers' house where the smaller kitchen was.

I walked in to the house not knowing what to expect. I tried to look back on the previous days to see where I could have gone wrong. I think it is embedded in you from childhood. When an older person calls you, you tend to think it has to be because of a mistake you made. I have never been called and thought they were going to congratulate you on something that you did right.

I think it is wrong that we approach conversations with those that are older than us in that way. I was surprised when all they wanted to know was the progress of my day.

They were like my parents now. They knew more about me at that moment than my actual parents. I started to feel like they were privy to thing was pulling at me earlier in the morning.

"Where have you reached with the school fess fund?" my grandfather asked.

I told him I was short seven thousand shillings. He proceeded to give me a lecture. He went on about how proud they were of me.

"You took a tough situation and made it better my child."

My grandmother told me that I had the power to change my destiny and education was a step in the right direction.

"I know the next semester is about to begin and we want you to join with this new batch."

I was shocked that they remembered the details of my school admission. I thought I was the only one obsessed with keeping track of the timelines.

My grandfather walked into their bedroom and walked out with an envelope. He took out some money and handed them over to me and said. "My grandson Mmbuka, God is faithful the church donated to me these money for your studies to the university". It sounded like a joke, but I was in tears again with thanks and praising Ooh God thank you for coming to my aid" The commitment of my church to push me to the next level reminded me that there was more to this life even if you remain a few seconds away to infinity.

I was in shock. I did not know how my face looked like at that moment. I did not know what to say. I kept opening my mouth trying to say something but no words were coming out.

"I know it does not reach your target but we believe in you."

That's all he said and they walked to their bedroom together.

"Goodnight," my grandmother said as she locked their bedroom door.

I wanted to cry. One half of me was saying I could not accept the money and the other half of me was already packing my bags. That was the ultimate sacrifice. When I looked at the money in my hands, I just could not believe it.

Him saying that he believed in me was like a validation. I needed someone else to remind me that my dreams were not just fantasies.

I had managed to save up 15,000 shillings in all the odd jobs I had in the period that I was in Itando. I had sacrificed so much in order to get to that amount. Every time I looked at the money I had kept hidden, I amazed at my resilience.

That night in my grandparents' living room was my day of transitioning. I needed to start thinking of what was next.

I went to sleep hoping that the next day would bring me more good news.

I left home early the next day without even seeing my grandparents. I did not want to be late for the job I got at Mheshimiwa.

When I arrived I just found the moving trucks parking outside the gate. The foreman was opening the gate. I went in before the trucks drove in.

The movers offloaded the contents of the truck and they left. The mheshimiwa had a lot of material properties and they were all brand new. The election period was drawing near and he needed to set up base.

"We have to wait for him and his wife to arrive so that you can know where everything goes."

He stepped away to receive a phone call. All I heard was the person on the other end of the phone being told to hurry up.

Almost instantaneously there was a hoot at the gate. I rushed to open the gate. The mheshimiwa drove in and parked at the corner because there was no space near the main door. And the garage door was still drying since it was painted the previous night.

He walked out of the car and he went to open the car door for the passenger on that side. It was his wife; she was dressed in casual clothes like someone who was ready to get her hands dirty.

They both shook my hands. They were affluent but did not try to impose that on the people around them.

"Are you ready to work?" the mheshimiwa asked.

"Yes sir."

The wife beckoned me to the house while the mheshimiwa remained outside with the foreman.

"We will start with kitchen, it seems to take the most time," she said while smiling.

It was easy to work with the lady of the house because she gave specific instructions. The other worker joined us when we were about to begin working on the living room. Now that we had more than one hand the work moved faster.

By around six in the evening the work was done.

"Don't worry about the mopping someone will do that when we move in tomorrow," she said.

We were all tired by that time. She brought in food for us before we left. Their generosity seemed genuine.

"Thank you so much for helping us today."

As we walked out the mheshimiwa called us to get our payment.

"Wait a minute young man, I want to talk to you."

I pointed at myself wondering whether it is me he meant. Then he nodded. I stood beside his car waiting for him to finish a phone call.

He startled me when he walked up to me and started speaking.

He laughed.

"I didn't mean to scare you."

"So I hear that you are planning on joining university soon."

He already had the information so I stayed silent.

"I commend you for working on getting your school fees."

He went on to state how he was impressed with me for going the extra mile.

"Most young men just give up and become busy bodies around their home."

It was awkward just standing there as someone heaped praises on you. I did not know what to say I return.

"Thank you, sir."

"You are the future of this village you might not see it now but you are."

He urged me to keep maintain the attitude I had.

"You are a self-made person young man."

He folded something and then placed it in my hand.

"When I get into the government come look for me."

He said that as he walked into his house. His wife was at the door waiting for him. I could see how she looked at him. It felt genuine. But what did I know? I believed my parents were happy only to find out that their closet was full of dirt laundry.

As soon as I got out of mheshimiwa's compound I checked my hand. He had given me three thousand shillings adding to the two thousand he had given me for the job.

I was five thousand shillings richer and I had extra money which I could use for my other needs. I did not feel comfortable getting handouts but I could not dismiss people who wanted to help. I did not want to think of the future after joining university. I did not want to think about where the money would come from for my upkeep. All I cared about was the fact that I had money for the first semester. The chips would fall wherever they wanted after they enrolled. The one thing I had learnt about myself was the fact that I was resilient.

The mheshimiwa won the electoral seat that year. I tried looking for him hoping I could get a bursary. However getting to him was not as easy as I thought. What would I tell his aides? I built his house before he won the seat. Any person could come up with that story. I gave up on looking for him but I believed that he cared for my success. I would make a difference in the town that made me who I am.

Chapter Five

Kibisu was a strong force. Even when he was younger it was hard not to notice him. He had plans and we would listen to him in awe. But life happens and your plans have to be shelved.

My elder brother had become a functional alcoholic. Drinking was his coping mechanism. That's how my mum put it. Just like my father. She did not say that with spite but with fear. She did not know what would become of him if he did not get a break through.

He had a job and he was doing his best. Half of the money went to the needs of my mother and my other siblings. I could not help him, which was a sad realization. I tried my best to send whatever I had but that meant it would take away from my tuition fees. Life can take its toll on you. I was disheartened because he was a man I looked up to. I still look up to for the sacrifices he made for my siblings and I. We tried to keep in touch but I was using my grandfathers phone to talk to my family and credit was not an essential commodity. He was a father figure to all of us.

I try to remember my father with so much fondness. I do not understand why and how we got there! Because my subconscious knew it but I didn't want to acknowledge it.

My father was a figment of my imagination. He was the language that framed my vision. That is the best description I could give. My mother was tough but caring. I always felt like my mother was against me because of the rules she enforced in the house. I was always in school so I did not get to see how hard it was for my mother to stay with my father.

After my father left I had so many questions. I knew that he was just the weekend parent but when he was around everything seemed perfect.

I kept asking my mum what had happened not knowing I was opening up more wounds for her.

I remember her saying she could not do this anymore. What did this represent?

I remember one night I was sitting with my brother Isinga

"Do you miss dad?"

And he told me not all the time. At that time Isinga was fifteen years old. I was amazed at his response.

"You were not here to see it all Mmbuka."

Isinga referred to our father as the fist. It was in the way he spoke. It did not matter whom he was speaking to, he felt like he was doing everyone a favor by just being there. His words would take the air right out of you. You would try to breath but he would keep choking until you became subdued.

His looks could dull your very existence. He had happy days and sad days. The sad days could bring all joy out of your body.

"Mum could not say a word without him flinching." He was the final say even in matters that he had no right to dispute. My mother was also opinionated and I could never imagine her cowering down to anyone. On the days that their arguing song did not work. She too could get her jabs in. When my brother was speaking I started to remember such moments that I had opted to bury in the back of my mind.

My father was the kind of man that commanded attention. Everyone else in the vicinity was just a dot that nobody would care to notice. Everything thing with him was a battle and he had to emerge the winner.

"There was a day that they fought hadi the landlord came to intervene," Isinga stated. He recounted the events and I started to fell like I was there when it happened.

"What is going on in there?" the landlord said.

"Nothing!"

"Open the door."

"Nothing is happening. We're just having a conversation."

"That is no way to talk to a woman, mzee."

"She is my wife and it's none of your business."

"And this is my house. You won't kill your wife in it."

When the man left, dad turned on mum. Yelling profanities at her. He left to go drinking. You could hear mum whispering.

"I can't be reduced to a speck, be in a place where this man silences my thoughts," she said.

"What happened next?" I asked. That same night my mum packed a few of our clothes and we left.

We went to her sister's place. I knew what was going on but the younger ones just thought it was a road trip.

"We should not go back," I told mum that night.

But they went back. My father came back home begging. He was a charmer it would be so easy for you to believe him. They went back home and everything seemed fine for a while.

"What were they fighting about?"

"Oh, just the fact that dad had another family in Gilgil."

Kirya said that as if it was a matter of common knowledge. I wanted to know more details but what right did I have asking my younger brother about things I was not privy to. I was away in boarding school when all this happened. Then I came back home for a period of one week and everything seemed normal. I would see my dad once or not at all during the period I was there. He was my hero because I had not seen what he was capable of.

I have other siblings somewhere in this world and now my father was free to be their father wherever he was. I had not noticed how older he looked when he spoke like that. Older not by his appearance but by the words he choose to use.

Then I realized that it was all in the mind. He was fifteen but he was not thinking like a child. There is this myth that I read through stating that seven is the age of reason? It seems like it is illogical so lets stick to fifteen. You could be fifteen and think like you are thirty years. That's how Kirya thought and it amazed me.

Why were they shielding me from this? Was it because I was more sensitive to things like that? Did they think I would be affected to a point where I could not handle it? I hated not being in the loop. But if I were in the loop what could I have done to change the matters at hand?

I had no right to be angry. I was wrong on so many levels. I was not sensitive to the situations my mother and my siblings were going through. I was in school peddling stories about how perfect my family was yet it was being held together by glue.

I remember when my father left. I was angry with my mother for not bringing him back. I did not voice out my anger but it was noted in how I treated her.

I was still holding on to the hope that my father would come back. In my mind all that was needed was an apology from my mum. Should I be mad that he did not come back? Or should I be mad that he ignored his responsibilities?

Learning about the things my mum had to go through. She is the hero and I never noticed because I was blinded by my father's superficial heroism. She would literally give us food of her plate so that we don't go hungry.

Chapter Six

I was ready to go to school. I called my mum telling her that I had enough money to enroll for the first semester. She was screaming. I was laughing. You could see the difference in those emotions but they both expressed what they truly felt.

Relief. Even if it was just for a split second they knew the new hurdles could be easier to deal with.

"God is faithful my child," she kept repeating those words. I wished I were there with her to see her reaction. And hug her. I missed those moments the most. As you grow older you realize that having your mum there is essential. I took her for granted when she was around me and now I long for her.

She was teary. I do not think she thought that this moment would come to pass.

"I am coming to take you for you first day."

She spoke with so much finality; I knew that I could not change her mind. Her word was king.

"You do know that this is not kindergarten mum."

She laughed.

"I do not care."

I know she would be sacrificing a lot just to go with me to my campus but for some selfish reason I could not bring myself to tell her not to follow me. That's the thing about my mother; once her mind was made up nothing could change it.

I would never forget the night I told her to go and get dad back.

"If you want him that much go get him yourself."

It shut me right up and I never brought it up again.

She is so strong; it took being away from her for me to even notice.

I had so little to my name at that point. As I was packing I realized that everything I owned could fit into one bag. That did not deter me for one second. I was so excited to be going to school. All I could think about was how the lecture halls would look like, the hostel, the cafeteria and the friends I would make.

I had this almost fanatical expectation of what university would look like. I thought that people were too grown to be worrying about what someone had or what they did not have. I knew that there were strikes because of various underlying issues but I though they could be solved in an instant. I was a bit detached from the world because by the time I got home from my errands I did not have the energy to listen to the news on the radio. All that mattered to me was that I had my admission letter and no one could take that away from me. It was my wake up call and my lullaby at night. If I did not have anything to look forward to. I would have turned into a drunkard.

A second before my eyes shut to the world I recognize it. There was a hint of confusion. I wanted to wave it a way. I was travelling the next day and I did not want anything to ruin that moment for me. I do not know what it was but maybe it was a warning that it would not be an easy journey.

That night for dinner my grandparents slaughtered a chicken for me. It was like my going away party.

"This will always be your home," my grandfather stated.

I could see my grandmother nod as he said those words.

"I know."

"Do not be ashamed of who you are and where you've come from," he added.

He went on to tell me that I would meet different people while I was in school but I should focus on who I am. He told me I was destined for greatness.

"Don't let the city life sway you."

We finished our dinner and they told me that they would pray for me before I left. Everything was happening so fast. I did not expect this moment to come to pass. The first few months I was in Itando, I was in denial.

Then my grandfather gave me the wakeup call I needed and I did not slow down even for one day.

"This is not a punishment the earlier you realize that the better for you," he said. I remember those words because I was in my room at that time. It was around ten in the morning and I was not awake. The word sunk in after a week and nothing could stop me after that.

Nairobi was a new feeling for me. A feeling I was not sure I like. It was a feeling that I needed to acclimate to. It was congested. You had to fight to get around. People did not have manners but they were so busy trying to get to where they wanted to be.

I remember when we younger coming to Nairobi was the ultimate goal. And I did come to Nairobi. I was in class eight just about to sit for my Kenya Certificate of Primary Education. I had never been to Nairobi and I was dying to go. My parents needed to pay two thousand in order for me to go to Nairobi. I did not know how to break that news to my parents. That weekend my father was around and I knew it would be easier to do it with both of them there.

I was not an only child and when you asked for things you had to consider the rest. In my head it felt like a splurge going to Nairobi even though it was a school trip. We were not poor but I thought it was a bit selfish on my part.

I decided to go on the offensive when I brought up the subject. My mum and dad were in the sitting watching the news.

"Mummy I won't be going to school next week."

Both my father and mother looked at me as if I had started taking drugs.

"What do you mean?" My dad asked.

"I thought we cleared your school fees last week," my mother added.

"Yes you did, my classmates will be going to Nairobi for a school trip."

"And you are not going?" they asked in unison.

"I want to go but they need two thousand first," I said stuttering.

"And?" my mother asked looking very angry.

I started to support my weight on the wall closer to my bedroom so that if things went south I could run.

"It's a lot of money."

"Who told you that?" my father asked.

I stayed silent because I did not have an answer for that.

"Your job is to ask, not to make conclusions," my father stated.

He told me that he will leave the money with my mother.

"Never think that we will never support the things you want Wangila," my mother stated.

"Go to sleep now."

I went to my room so happy. It took a while before I could finally go to sleep. At that moment I realized that I had hurt my parent's feelings. I knew then that they would support me as long as they were able to. Well my mother that is because my father walked away when we needed him the most.

I wondered what in his psyche changed when he left us. He was always supportive and available for us. Then all of a sudden he could not even send money for a packet of flour.

We were going to be in Nairobi for three days. My mother packed my clothes for me. She took me to school on Monday and paid for my trip. On the travelling day she even gave me pocket money.

"Have fun my son."

She waved at me as the bus drove away; my father was already in Gilgil for work. There was bucket list that one had to check when they arrived in the big city. Sarit center, Giraffe center and the national park. Your trip would be incomplete if you did not visit these places.

I was in complete awe especially when I got to Sarit center. It was one of the biggest shopping malls I had ever seen in my life. I used the escalator for the first time and it felt like I was touching heaven. I was raised in Nakuru which was the cleanest town at one point. Even though it was a town that was growing, infrastructure was still not up to par. There were so many things I had not seen at that point. I was not excited about the animals because we had the Lake Nakuru National park in our town then. The buildings were the highlight of my trip, that and sleeping away from home. We ate junk food the whole time we were there.

I talked about that trip till my siblings asked me to shut up. I would repeat it in different versions. It all depended on who I was talking to. I just needed them to know that I had been to Nairobi. Some people would be intrigued by my experience but some people had been there before. It did not matter to them as much as it did.

This time I was going to Nairobi to embark on a new journey. I was excited about the journey but not so excited about the location.

I was with my mother as we approached the University of Nairobi. I had my one bag with countable things in it and my mother was carrying a kikoy with things she thought I needed.

If anyone looked at me I felt like they could see through me because I was so excited. I was finally here. We had arrived by half past seven in the morning. This was during the time we could travel at night without any hindrance.

Chapter Seven

I left Itando and I looked back thanking it for the person it made me. I was ready to conquer the world because every experience I had there. My grandparents prayed for me and I remembered every word. They spoke so many things that I wanted to come into existence.

"I will make you proud," I said as I waved them goodbye. My grandmother cried but I promised to come back. I knew that it was my home. I could not go back to my mother's house because it would not be enough for the rest of the children who were with her.

I met my mother in Nakuru when we made a stopover after agreeing on my grandfather phone to meet their. Our reunion was filled with so much emotion. We were crying. I am sure the by standers were wondering what was going on.

"You have grown my boy."

"It hasn't been that long mum."

She just held me. Looking to see if there were parts of me that were broken and she could not see.

"I had to do it Wangila."

"Mum you don't have to explain anything, I understand completely."

We talked about my siblings and what they have been up to since I last saw them. She had no pictures to show me but she told me that they had written something for me. I am sure she forced them to do that but I was excited to read through them nonetheless. Inyaya was just a baby when I left but now she was starting school. I was missing out on their milestones but I was making a promise to myself to be more involved.

"I will give them to you later."

The rest of the journey was uneventful. We were asleep half the time. Nakuru to Nairobi was a two and half hour journey.

I looked at my mother. The wrinkles on her face were her battle scars. She was fighting to stay afloat and it was taking everything including her youth. I could not wait to be able to carry some of the burden that she had.

We walked to the admission office to sort my school issues. We had to wait a while for the attendants to arrive before we could be sorted.

When they finally arrived we were the first people in line. I had to explain that I was admitted earlier but was not able to attend.

They checked the details I had presented just to verify what I had said. It took a while because it was in the archives. Things were not digitized during this period. They were trying to do that but it was done on recent admissions.

"Mmbuka here are your documents," she stated.

I was directed to the finance office in order to finalize my admission. I had paid the required amount to the bank. It was stamped and they gave me details for the next semester.

"How can I get the HELB loan?"

They gave me a pamphlet to read through before I could make a definite decision. I went back to the admissions office which housed the rooms section. I showed them my stamped receipt and they gave me a room.

"You'll get a key once you talk to the resident assistant in your building."

They asked me to show the resident assistant the document they had handed over to me. I had come a week after orientation and therefore I had to navigate my way around without any assistance.

Saying goodbye to my mother was hard because I had not seen her in a while. The short time we spent together just showed me how much I had missed spending time with her.

She handed me a phone.

"Mama I can't take this."

"I need to be able to know how you are doing. It doesn't look like much but this is all I could afford."

In Itando I used my grandfather's phone. It was out of charge most of the time and we never had credit. I had not thought about owning one but my mum made me realize that I needed one.

She helped me locate my hostel. I felt like a child at that moment and I did not want to let her go.

"You will be fine my child."

I wanted to say I knew that but instead I hugged her.

"We will figure everything out together," she said. She prayed for me before she left. As she walked away I knew that I had to work hard for her. She had given up so much for me and she was willing to give up even more. A mother's love is undisputed and no one knows the lengths it is willing to go. I knew my mother would give up her own life for my siblings and me.

I walked into the building that would be my home for the next four years. It was very confusing as I walked in because I could see a couple of girls walking around. I walked out again to confirm the details on my slips. I looked around for the resident assistant's office so that I could get my key. I found it easily because I was told it was on the first floor.

I knocked before I went in. I explained everything to him and he sorted me out.

"You are very lucky to get a room past orientation."

I later on learnt that rooms were a hot commodity on campus. Seniors would sell their rooms just to make some extra cash.

I walked to my room which was on the third floor. I walked in to find three other guys in the room. I said hello to them but they were pre-occupied with other things.

I noticed that the top bank was unoccupied and placed my things there. They were using a laptop. The first I had ever seen. I thought it was a computer. Once they finished what they were doing they were very pleasant. We exchanged names and they gave the details of how living with them would be.

I was the only freshman in that room but I knew that I would be able to get along with them.

The first point of order was exile. I had heard about with Bwire but I had thought it was a dwindling culture. They were very serious about it. Not to sound pessimistic they seemed like the guys that did not get any girls in their room. I just nodded in respect. I knew that I would be staying away from girls until I finished my course because I did not need or want any distractions.

I was given one cupboard to put in my belongings. I arranged my things neatly as they walked out to get dinner.

I opened the box containing the phone. It was just a simple phone that could perform the necessary functions texting, sending money and calling. But in the box my mum had put in some money for me. I could not help but smile. I was only left with two thousand after sorting the tuition fees and all my campus needs. I set up the phone and texted my mother immediately to say thanks.

That was the room I stayed in till I finished campus. I had different roommates but I was a constant feature in room 307. I would have moved to another room but I like the consistency that I felt while I was there. It felt like home because I could not go back to Itando as often as I would have liked to.

Moving out of the hostel was not an option for me because I could not pay the rent without straining myself. I had to think of eating, ensuring that I could get study materials and navigate my way through Nairobi if need be.

Chapter Eight

My first week in campus was a delight. I think I was the only freshman so excited to be there. It was something I had been counting down to for a while. I never missed class. If I was not in class I was in the library. I was always reading. My classmates would call me the guy with all the answers. They just did not understand that I could not be walking around with them. I could not afford their lifestyle. I was in the class with parallel students because of the time I joined.

I was not sacred about being in campus just a bit nervous. I was ready to conquer the world. But the world was a bit different from how I remembered it.

I was from upcountry and so many things had happened that I was not aware of. In terms of technology but that did not deter me. I could learn. I was willing to learn because it seemed it had become an essential part of how the world navigated.

I remember when one of my roommates asked me whether I was on Facebook. In my head I wondered what the hell that was.

But more advances came and I was part of it. Just because you were not a part of something at one point does not mean that you cannot catch up. There was twitter, whatsapp and instagram. Time would never stand still. It will move on without waiting for you to catch up. If you want to catch up you have to run after it but it would still be ahead of you. Time is the very definition of unrequited love you pray for it to stay but you have no choice when it walks away.

I was even ridiculed for my dressing but I could not afford to let that get in my ahead. I had no money to start thinking that I could start buying clothes every day.

Then I discovered Gikomba market. It had everything I needed but I had to do a deep dive before I could get anything. That is where my first business started as I tried to make money. I was in second year by then. It was an untapped market. The boys in my campus did not want to be found ransacking through a bunch of clothes or shoes. They were happy to have someone do it for them. I was not ashamed to do it. They would just come and make an order and I would go to Gikomba and find what they were looking for.

It failed somewhere in the middle because I had so much work to do at school and I could not keep up with the demands of my market. I survived with that business through my second year and third year. The HELB loan I used to get was just enough for the school fees, sending a bit to mother and my grandparents and my upkeep. It was not enough for the Nairobi scene.

Campus was the hub of diversity for me. You were provided with so many options. Peer pressure was a factor that influenced your choices even though we would like to deny it. I did not have that luxury because this was a matter of life or death for me. If I messed up my life in campus that would mean going back to Itando to start laying bricks again. I wanted more out of life.

There were guys with no direction or guidance on what to do. They had so many questions that were filled with illusions but lacked direction. I had set my standards of perfection and there was no room for failure .It was either I made it or I failed. Failure was not an option. When I was in third year right after my second hand clothes business failed my roommate tried to recruit me into a group they had. They always had money and I was attracted to that. They would outside campus and the only thing I could afford was a meal at the mess that would cost a maximum of seventy shillings.

I thought they were dealing in electronics because of the different brands they had often. My roommate kept that room just to show the mum that he was in school. He was a troubled kid from the stories I gathered.

I found out they were selling drugs, I could not get out of that room fast enough. Marijuana was their main moneymaker. I was desperate for money but I was not willing to become a criminal for it.

"Why did you rush out like that?" my roommate asked.

I looked at him confused because I thought it was self-explanatory.

"Drugs Mike?"

He sat on his bed laughing but I was getting angry.

"What you do on your own time is your business don't involve me," I stated.

"Don't be dramatic Wangila, I thought you wanted money."

"I wanted money but not in that way."

"Be easy my guy I was just trying to hook you up," he stated.

I wasn't even mad at him. I was just scared I saw my life flashing before me and all I could see was prison. I know I was being dramatic but I wanted to live an honest life. He bought me dinner that night. Mike was a cool guy and I knew that he did not have any ill intentions. He thought he was looking out for me. We laughed about it when we met after campus.

Chapter Nine

Third year was a year for change for me. I wanted to change my campus even in the smallest way. I vied for a student leader position as the deputy chairperson administration and finance. I wanted to change how dissemination of funds was being conducted within the campus. My few friends told me that I was being too ambitious but I wanted to try. That is where my interest in politics was planted.

I did not have money to have a splashy campaign but that did not deter me. I was surprised at how courageous I was. I have never been an outspoken person but when it came to things I was passionate about nothing could shut me up.

People would ask me what I would give to them if they voted for me. My answer was that I would bring change because that was all I had to offer. Many would laugh at me. They took every opportunity to tell me that I would loose. The thing was that I did not mind loosing; I would be disappointed in myself if I did not put up a big fight.

"You cannot carry out fundamental change without a certain amount of madness. In this case, it comes from nonconformity, the courage to turn your back on the old formulas, the courage to invent the future. It took the madmen of yesterday for us to be able to act with extreme clarity today. I want to be one of those madmen. We must dare to invent the future."

That was part of my speech; I quoted Thomas Sankara the late president of Burkina Faso. I urged my fellow students to join the movement of madmen who wanted to make a difference. I said those words with so much conviction; I used the same words as I made my debut in national politics as a member of parliament.

I think the reason I won was because of my manifesto. I wanted to make changes that could be visible across the divide. I did not make unrealistic promises; I stated facts that were clear as day to everyone in the campus community. I didn't have money to throw around I just had policies that I believe should have changed. I wanted to bring equality for all the students across the divide. I had learnt that true equality lacks resentment. But there was resentment amongst the students and that's what I needed to work on.

I was a campus leader who shunned corruption and it was for that reason that I was ousted after serving one term. Campus politics was a dirty game. I played it and won. I did it differently. My fellow leaders wanted to hide a bit of money dedicated for student activities, I would refuse. I was a goody two shoes. I knew that if we took a small amount it would affect the activities set out for the semester. I would not allow it. Once the funds were not enough they would take that opportunity to blame it on the administration. It was hard to work under those conditions but when I left office I was proud of what I had achieved. I wished I could have done more but you need to have a community that is willing to work with you as you progress. They wanted to enrich themselves and I wanted to leave a legacy behind.

I was grateful for the experience that I got. I was also very grateful because they would be a subsidy on my tuition fees. Working with the student body made me realize that if I wanted to make a difference I would have to work

harder than everyone else.

Chapter Ten

What is a story without a love anecdote in it? I met girl while I was in campus. She was the epitome of what perfection looked like. She was intelligent that was what attracted me to her. She was beautiful as well but it did not come close to her mind. She was in the engineering school. I met just as I was about to graduate. I had girlfriends before but they left me as soon as they realized that I did not have money. Mawondo was different and I didn't deserve her. I pretended that my feelings towards her were platonic. What did I have to offer her?

She came from an affluent family but she was not bourgeois. She was down to earth and I told her everything about my life. She never judged me and I liked her for that. She was one of my best friends. I wanted to be more than friends but I could not even take care of myself. That was the first time I ever felt truly in love. She made me feel vulnerable and I was not ashamed of that vulnerability. I never told her I was in love with her. I could not start lying to her that I would give her the universe when I did not know where my next meal would be coming from.

We lost touch after I graduated because I went back to Itando but she always kept in touch. I did not have enough money to keep calling her. It did not end in spite just something that could be rekindled once we were in the same environment.

I graduated with a second upper class distinction. Which was an accolade. I was disappointed because I did not get first-class honors.

No one in my family was able to attend my graduation. Even Kibisu who was in Nairobi could not make it because his wife had just given birth. My mother was dealing with my younger siblings who were about to finish their Kenya Certificate of Secondary Education.

Mawondo was the only one there for me. I loved that. She took me out for lunch in a fancy restaurant. She celebrated my success even though I had not been able to get a job immediately after graduation.

"Things will look up Wangila don't let this shake you," Mawondo stated as she hugged me goodbye.

I stayed in Nairobi for about a week to try and find a job. I could not stay past that because I did not have money to cater for my stay there. I missed the security that the hostel provided me.

The dynamics of me being a degree holder did not change the fact that the world did not realize that. Jobs were not just being handed to everyone just because I had a degree. It took a second for me to realize that. I had this notion that once I graduated. All my chips would fall into place. No one warns you on what you'd have to go through in order to have just one piece of the puzzle in the right place.

I went back to Itando to regroup. That is what I decided to call it because I was not going back to leech of my grandparents.

It was the age of the Internet and I would go to the only cyber café we had in Itando to apply for jobs. Ayira would send me jobs to apply via text. I had upgraded my phone to the cheapest smartphone I could get because I needed to be online. When I started getting calls for jobs I knew that I had to head back to the city. I had saved up some money working in that cyber café I knew I could be able to at least sustain myself for a month.

I tarmacked before I finally got a job. It would be a lie to say that it was easy. In some interviews they would tell you that I had to work for free before they started paying me. I would have loved to just get experience but I needed money. I did not have the luxury of asking someone to cater to my bills.

I was almost giving up but Mawondo kept encouraging me. She was still in school but she was about to finish. I was living in a single room in Kibera with the basic necessities. I could not even afford to cook for myself because it would increase my budget.

I remember the first time Mawondo visited me in that room. She had bought so many things for me. She had always been selfless. If she wanted to help nothing you said could stop her.

She did not look at my humble abode in disgust. Instead we made jokes about it. It was that same day she visited me that I landed a clerical job in a logistics company associated with AIM body.

"You see I am your good luck charm Mmbuka," she said.

And she was. It was during this period that I fell in love with her more. She saw something in me that I might not have seen myself.

I was working hard for my family and for her. I wanted to be a better man for her. Nairobi is not an easy city to live in especially without a significant salary. My clerical job felt like the light at the end of the tunnel. I was earning fifteen thousand shillings, which was enough during that period. I was able to save some and I was able to send back home.

I took Mawondo out on a date with my first salary. It was not anything fancy just a simple lunch in one of the most expensive fast food joint. Well it was expensive according to me.

Seeing that smile on her face was enough for me. I should have already told her I wanted to be with her bit I had to make something of myself first.

Life in Nairobi gets harder especially if you have to pay bills and use transportation. There were days I would walk from my house to the office so that I save even a coin. I was determined to brave through this hurdle just as I had braved through all the other challenges.

I was starting to feel comfortable with my position at the logistics company. I was starting to make friends. It was then that everything came tumbling down.

I went to the office one day and people were clearing the documentation in the office. I was given a check for half my salary.

I was stunned. I could not believe that I was back to the unemployment lane. I found out later on that the donors who were funding the organization withdrew their support because of misappropriation of funds.

I felt dejected because that meant starting the job search all over again. I was lucky that I had been saving. I felt bad for the people with families who had no other source of income.

After a month I realized that a job would not fall on my lap just because of a University degree. I started hawking sweets along the streets of Nairobi. The Lang'ata area was my route.

It felt like a downward spiral but I had no choice. I could not tell my family that I lost my job and I was now a hawker. Hawking was not an easy task there were days I would go home with nothing. I would sit on my bed and wonder when I would get a break through. It was hard. I would wake up very early in the morning to target the commuters heading to work. If I started my day in the afternoon I would not make a lot of money.

Hawking sweets was not sustaining my needs so I started vending newspapers. I would wear my suit in the morning and someone would think that I was going to some big organization. I would go to various distributors and get my newspapers for the day.

I walked in to various offices and poached some clients. I was the guy who delivered their newspapers. I became close with people from top management and that's how things turned around for me. They always wondered how an educated man like me was doing such work. My answer was always you make do with the thing you have and hope for better.

One of the guys asked for my curriculum vitae during one of my deliveries. I did not hesitate to give it to him. I always walked around with my curriculum vitae just in case something came up.

The newspaper-vending job helped me to network, which was a good thing for me. I met people who wanted to help me and I met people who treated me badly just because of my description.

"Hi Mmbuka, you deliver newspapers at our offices in town can we have a meeting tomorrow?"

That was the call that changed my life. Those words gave me hope even though they did not say much.

I went to the Cyberport international offices in the central business district. I wore my best suit that day and that was not saying much.

I sat down in a panel for an interview. I was very nervous because I could not believe that I was there. In one of the biggest companies I had ever been to. They had systems in place that gave you security unlike my previous place of employment.

I landed the job with Cyberport International Logistics Company. The interview was not as intense as I had expected but they did a thorough background check on who I was and where I had worked before.

I did not lie about where I had come from and they were impressed with my work ethic. The manager at Cyberport did not owe me anything. But when he recommended me for the job even though I used to deliver their newspapers, I was touched.

This was my turning point. Immediately I got the job I called Mawondo

"I got the job Mawondo."

"Congratulations Mmbuka I knew you could do it."

I could hear the joy in her voice. She had graduated and was now working for a top engineering firm. What amazed me about her is the fact that she never looked down on me. No matter which point I was in my life.

"I have one more thing to tell you, I want to be with you."

I do not know where I got the courage from but I finally told her how I felt. I thought to myself there would never be the perfect moment. I could loose her to someone else as I waited for it.

"Took you long enough," she said while laughing.

That is how our relationship blossomed.

Chapter Eleven

Working at Cyberport International helped me progress my life. I was earning enough money to sustain my life. I moved out of my single room house to a one-bedroom house in Lang'ata.

After staying there for over four years. I was promoted to a better position in the same company. This then changed the dynamics of my life.

I started by upgrading my grandparent's farm back in Itando. I bought chicken and farm equipment so that the farm could sustain itself. I hired farm help in order to assist them with the duties at home. This was able to provide income for them as well as myself. I was giving back to the people that raised me.

I opened posho mills in the area to provide employment for the young people in the area. I wanted to do more for that community.

My mother was so happy for my success. I was able to help her with my brothers and sister that was my biggest priority. I was able to rent a house for her so that she could live in a better situation. I wanted to build her a house but I could not afford to do it at that moment.

I remember the day that I introduced Mawondo to my family. She fit in immediately. She got along with my mother and that was interesting to witness. We were growing as a couple and friends. I loved that about us we were from different divides. When I went to her home for the first time I was amazed. They were wealthy but she never threw that money in anyone's face. We had been dating for around three years then and we wanted to get married. I felt like I had entered in an alternate universe. Her family received me with open arms that enabled me to feel confident about my request.

Mawondo was the epitome of confidence and that was attributed to her family. She shared in my passion of trying to change the world in anyway we could. We tried to volunteer work just to do our share in society. I had met people who had been kind to me my grandparents, the foreman, mheshimiwa, my mother, the manger at Cyberport International and Mawondo herself. I wanted to share the love that had been handed over to me.

We had been married for around two years when I told Mawondo that I wanted to get into politics. We had two children then. He was watching television while sitting on the floor.

" I want to be an MP in Sabatia which housed my Village Itando."

"You seem so certain about it?" she asked me.

I laughed. She looked at me wondering why I was laughing.

"I am not certain but I want to try," I stated.

We had an in-depth conversation on the matter. We stated the pros and cons of being in the public eye.

"I am going to support you my love," she stated as we slept.

I decided to embrace politics. I had my ties in Itando and decided that would be the place I would begin my political career.

I had set base at my grandparent's house and people remembered me from when I was a young boy. The political period was not easy on my family but they knew who I was and that ensured that we stayed firm in our relationships.

I used the same strategy that I employed as I vied for the political seat in campus. I did not make promises I could not fulfill. My track record spoke for itself. Even without a political seat I tried to bring hope to my community.

"We will vote for you because we have seen you grow."

Those were the words I heard as I was on the ground. I could not let them down because they believed in me.

I wanted Itando which is part of Sabatia to keep up with the rest of the country. We had a long way to go but that did not shake me.

Chapter Twelve

The night the results were being announced; I remember the generator ran out of fuel. We all began to yell because we were nervous. One of my brothers rushed to the market to get fuel because we did not have any supply in the house.

It was a nerve wrecking experience. I had people on the ground but they could not give me conclusive results. They told me that we were neck to neck with my opponent. I was prepared that for whatever outcome but a win would be a good thing for me.

We were all restless. I was walking around the house-making phone calls until my phone went off. It was around nine when I could hear music outside drumbeats and feet rushing towards our house.

"Mmbuka ni wetu!" (Mmbuka belongs to us)

People rushed out of the house. I could not move, I thought I was imagining the whole situation.

"Babe you won," Mawondo stated. That is how I came back to reality. She pulled me outside. I thought I was imagining my grandparents dancing but they were outside screaming my name.

When people realized that I was outside they all rushed towards me. Then I was no longer on the ground. My constituents lifted me up while singing my praises. I would not let that get to my head because if I failed to deliver my downfall would be documented in an even bigger manner.

My life flashed before me. I could not believe that I was the same person who would work for minimum pay just to ensure that I was able to get by. I was determined not to let my people down.

I looked around and even though it was dark I could see my family. My mother was kneeling down praying because that was how she got through the tough times. Praying for my life and that of my brothers.

For a second I thought about my father. I wondered whether he saw me and recognized me as his son. I wondered what would happen if he would try to get in touch with me.

Those thoughts were interrupted when I was put on the ground. Mawondo and my children rushed to hug me.

"You did it Mmbuka," she whispered in my ear.

I stayed true to my word to bring change to Itando and the larger Sabatia. Infrastructure was a big bone of contention in the area by the time I took that seat and I was going to remedy it.

With the funds I got from the government I was able to ensure that the projects were being done. Some of the projects had been started by my predecessors by word of mouth only. I had to look back on those issues as well.

I tried to have an open door policy with my constituents so that I could represent them better when I went to Nairobi for parliamentary proceedings.

I ensured that electricity was brought the village to ensure that people could work at night without fear of the darkness.

My biggest achievement in my opinion was the tertiary college that I started. It was open to people within the region and those seeking education from other areas. I made sure to reward students who were brilliant but could not afford to pay their fees. This enabled the people to know that there are alternative means of getting income if you get exposed to different environments.

I was recognized as one of the best performing Member of Parliament. It was not an accolade that I so desired because I was doing my job. I had become a mad man that wanted to change the future of my people. Through this I was called for an interview to talk about how I was able to do that. I hated the fact that this was something we were discussing. I was a leader first; power should not influence how you behave towards people. Certain people used to tell me I was overworking. There were places that I failed the people because they expected some results immediately. I was not perfect and I did not want to present that picture.

It was during that interview where the panel retrieved photos of me hawking sweets. I looked at that picture and I could not believe that it was me.

"That is an old photo," I stated. You never truly know what the river will bring down the stream.

It was obvious it was old but stating it just made realize how far I had come from. We talked about that picture and all the things I had to go through to be there at that moment.

"Nothing is set on stone you have the power to change it, you just have to want it," I stated as the interview was coming to an end.

I further added that it was not meant to be an easy journey but you have to take it a step at a time. I mean if I was looking in from the outside I would not believe that I had made it thus far.

"I want to vie for governor in my next term in that way I will impact more people," I said.

Nothing was holding me back all I had to do was dream it and I could achieve it. I had to work hard. Just because I was in an influential position did not mean that things would be easy for me.

It would be too obvious to state that people had written me off. It was the actual opposite so many people believed in me. I think that was why I was able to make it. The fact that I knew people had faith in me even when I was at my wits end made me standup and fight another day.

I finally got to build my mother that house that she always wanted. The look on her face gave me peace. That day she sent me a way to my grandparents' home might have been my worst day ever. I look back and think but what if I stayed?

My modest beginnings never came in the way of my dreams. I think that it was I wanted to be written down in history. I am who I am because of the people who directed me in my path to success.

"Do you think money changed you?"

I remember when someone asked me that question. Did I have a definite answer? I think mumbled something about it not changing me but looking back I lied.

Money did change me. It opened doors for me and my community that I could only dream of. I had never been to an airport but now I could see the world on a whim. I do not take it for granted. Being able to provide for my family and those that depend on me is a delight. People wanted to be associated with me now that I was affluent; it is not something I am proud of. It only made me realize that you can trust people as far as you can throw them. The best thing about the success I enjoy now is the fact that I can make a difference. That's why I ventured into politics. I did not do it for the power; I did it so that I can be a leader. My character did not change when I was put it in a position of power it helped me compartmentalize situations. I could sympathize with the plight of people and also know where to draw the line.

I have experienced life on both sides of the divide. Not so many people get to do that. I know what it feels like to lack and I know what it feels like to have in excess. That luxury is what helps me do better to ensure that I help out where I can. I fall too. I fell before but I do not let it bring me down. I use that energy to pick myself and make my self stronger.

THE END